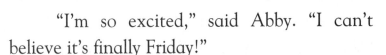

"I'm so excited," said Abby. "I can't believe it's finally Friday!"

"Woof," agreed Tess.

"We must be nearly there." Abby glanced down at the directions scribbled on the scrap of paper in her hand. "I know it's on this street."

Tess yipped and grinned broadly. She trotted along beside Abby, her blue eyes bright with anticipation.

Abby sighed inwardly and hoisted the strap of her backpack higher on her shoulder. Her little sister Tess was well known for being quirky. "Unique" was the word Mom used. Weird was more like it, Abby thought, but she had learned not to let it bother her. After awhile you got used to a sister who barked and howled and chewed on a rubber dog bone. Besides, she was way too excited to let Tess's canine behavior bug her today.

Because today was Friday and they were

on their way to a pet-sitting job.

Abby slowed her steps and looked more carefully at the numbers on the houses. "I can't believe we got a job so soon," she said to Tess. "We've only had our poster up for a week."

Abby had made the poster herself. It was bright and colorful, with drawings of cats and dogs and rabbits all around the edges. Right in the middle, written in big, bold letters, were the words "Going away? Need someone to look after your pet? Call Abby and Tess. We're responsible and reliable and our rates are reasonable."

Jeremy, who owned the pet store near their apartment building, had said she and Tess could tack up their poster on the store's bulletin board. A few days later Mr. Maggioli had called. He was a friend of Jeremy's. He even knew their mom from the art class she taught at the community center.

Abby had been pretty nervous when Mom handed her the phone. After all, Mr. Maggioli was her first real client. But he was nice. He invited Abby and Tess to come by on Friday after school so he could introduce them to his pet lizard, Angus.

Their first official pet-sitting job! Well, it was actually Abby's second pet-sitting job. Her first had been looking after Mrs. Wilson's two goldfish, Speedy and Slowpoke, while she was away for a week.

Mrs. Wilson lived down the hall in the same building as Abby and Tess. The building was old and had too many stairs and Abby didn't like living there. The hallways smelled funny, especially at suppertime when everyone was cooking something different. The people who lived in the apartment below them played boring opera music at night when Abby wanted to sleep. And worst of all, there was that dumb rule: No Pets Allowed.

Abby loved animals, all kinds of animals. She was going to be a veterinarian when she grew up just so she could be around them all day long. That's why she'd wanted to look after Mrs. Wilson's goldfish. To get some practice. She'd done such a good job that Mom had said she could start her very own pet-sitting business. And Tess could be her helper. It was a brilliant plan!

"I wonder what kind of lizard Angus is," she said out loud. "Mr. Maggioli didn't mention it on the phone."

She had looked in all her animal books to learn about the different kinds of lizards people kept as pets. Iguanas, chameleons, geckos . . . there were so many. A boy at school had a bearded dragon, which didn't even sound like a kind of lizard. To be honest, lizards weren't her idea of fun pets. Still, a job was a job.

Tess halted abruptly to bark at a gray and white cat perched atop a fence post. The cat viewed Tess through half-closed eyes, unconcerned. Tess barked one last time and then ran to catch up with Abby.

"Angus," Abby said again, ignoring Tess and the cat. It was a windy afternoon and she paused to zip up her windbreaker. "It's kind of a funny name, don't you think? Sounds like a cow. But I guess you wouldn't give a lizard a name

like Fluffy or Cuddles."

Tess giggled. They walked along for a few more minutes, then Abby stopped. She looked at the address on the paper and studied the house in front of them. It was painted a friendly yellow and had flower boxes under the windowsills. Tiny blue blossoms filled the flower boxes and spilled over the sides.

Abby took a deep breath. "This is it," she said. She turned to Tess. "Ready?"

Tess nodded.

"Okay. Let's go ring the doorbell." Abby put one hand on the gate, then halted. "And remember," she added, looking directly into Tess's eyes. "Let me do the talking, okay?"

"Woof!"

2 Hide and Seek

"Come in, girls," said Mr. Maggioli, taking their coats. "Angus is right through here."

Abby and Tess followed him down a wide hallway lined with paintings. They were mostly of bowls of fruit and Abby guessed that Mr. Maggioli had painted them himself. He was a tall man, with shaggy hair and wire glasses that sat high on his long, bony nose. He led them past the kitchen and through the living room, which had an elegant black piano in one corner.

"I thought it might be a good idea to introduce you to him before I leave," Mr. Maggioli said over his shoulder as he walked. "Lizards are often nervous around new people. Quite nervous, in fact. But if you're patient and gentle with them, they usually calm down. Ah, here we are."

They entered a cluttered, comfortable room. Abby guessed it was a study. A highly polished wooden desk sat in the middle, taking up most of the floor space. Tall, sturdy shelves stuffed with books and papers lined the walls. And in the far corner, on a squat, round table, sat Angus. Or rather, a big glass box.

Oh no, thought Abby, not another aquarium!

She remembered all too well what had happened the last time Tess got near an aquarium. Now here they were, another pet-sitting job and another aquarium. She wasn't sure she liked the looks of this.

"Come closer, girls," urged Mr. Maggioli. "I want you to meet a special friend of mine."

Abby hesitated, then stepped toward the low table. Tess followed behind her like a shadow. The glass tank looked much the same as Mrs. Wilson's aquarium, but instead of containing water, it held earth and rocks and living, growing plants.

"It looks like a jungle in there," Abby said.

Mr. Maggioli nodded approvingly. "Oh yes, very good. That's exactly what it is. A vivarium. A miniature jungle. It's the perfect environment for Angus."

Abby studied the vivarium. The lid wasn't hinged, like an aquarium lid would be. It was solid, and it was made entirely of glass. She leaned forward and noticed droplets of moisture clinging to its underside. In one corner a tall plant with spiky leaves reminded her of the spider plant that hung over the kitchen sink at home. Miniature ferns sprouted up behind small logs and rocks and fuzzy green moss grew in

patches here and there. The damp earth was covered in some places with gravel and loose sand. On one side sat a large, flat rock under a glowing spotlight.

But there was no lizard. Abby and Tess exchanged puzzled glances.

"Are you sure he's in there?" asked Abby. "I don't see him."

Mr. Maggioli chuckled. "Yes, absolutely. Angus is most certainly in there. But he can be hard to spot because of his coloring, and he loves to hide."

Abby stared through the glass, but the vivarium seemed empty.

"There he is," Mr. Maggioli said. He pointed to a knobby branch with rough brown bark. The branch was almost as long as the aquarium. Its thick end was wedged into the earth and its thin end leaned at an angle against the glass. But even with the help of Mr. Maggioli's finger, Abby couldn't spot Angus.

Suddenly Tess yipped excitedly. She turned to Abby and grinned. "I see him!"

3 Sneak Attack

Abby frowned. Tess panted and pointed at the branch, but as far as Abby could tell, it was empty. Then it shifted and she saw that it wasn't just a branch after all. A thin lizard with a pointy head and a long, skinny tail was clinging to the wood.

"He looks exactly like the bark," she said with a delighted smile.

Angus gazed at them through the glass. Abby stared back, charmed. He was so tiny and cute. From the tip of his nose to the end of his tail, he was no longer than Abby's hand. He looked exactly like a little kid's toy.

"Well, he's not always brown," Mr. Maggioli told them. "He can also be green. It depends on his mood and the temperature."

Abby's eyes lit up. "He's a chameleon?"

"No, no," Mr. Maggioli shook his head and smiled. "But you're close. Angus is a green anole. Anoles are actually related to iguanas, but they can change color just like chameleons. An extremely interesting species."

"Green anole," Abby repeated. She frowned. "I don't remember reading about them."

Mr. Maggioli took off his glasses and cleared his throat noisily. "Well, they're pretty common lizards in warm-climate countries. You can easily find them in the southern United States and the Caribbean. Places like that. They like the sun. People often see them lying on rocks or climbing on houses, looking for a warm spot. Which reminds me, Angus is an excellent climber, so I'm very careful to keep the lid on at all times."

"Can I hold him?" asked Tess.

He looked uncertain. "I don't know, Tess. Anoles aren't always that friendly. I mean, they're usually pretty calm, but sometimes . . ." He hesitated, then put his glasses back on. "Why don't I take him out of the tank so you can touch him?"

Tess panted eagerly. Abby knew that if her sister were really a dog, her tail would be wagging like crazy right now.

They watched Mr. Maggioli slide the lid to one side, leaving a narrow opening. Angus lay motionless on the branch. He stared straight ahead as Mr. Maggioli cautiously lowered his hand into the tank. But as the hand closed around him, Angus suddenly whipped his head sideways and sank his teeth into Mr. Maggioli's finger.

Tess yelped.

Mr. Maggioli smiled weakly. Abby noticed his eyes were watering, but he didn't release Angus. Gently, he cupped Angus with his free hand and lifted him out of the tank. Angus glared at them, his thin tail whipping back and forth angrily. His teeth remained firmly embedded in the finger.

"I thought this might happen," Mr. Maggioli said, holding the lizard close to his chest. "Angus and I are still getting to know each other. I've only had him for a few weeks, you know. I'm hoping we'll soon become friends."

The girls watched him stroke the lizard's

back, which was now more green than brown. Mr. Maggioli began to croon softly. Gradually Angus relaxed. After a minute he let go of Mr. Maggioli's finger. Two tiny spots of blood popped up where his teeth had been.

"I think he's calm now," Mr. Maggioli said. "Would you like to pet him?"

Suddenly Abby didn't think Angus looked all that cute anymore. Nervously, she shook her head. She felt Tess press close to her. Tess was probably having second thoughts too. This job might not be as much fun as they had thought. But it was only for the weekend. Two days.

They could look after one tiny lizard for two days, couldn't they?

4 A Piece of Cake

"I thought I'd take notes," said Abby quickly. Her desire to touch Angus had disappeared. She pulled a notebook out of her backpack. "What exactly do you want us to do?"

Mr. Maggioli gently set Angus on his branch. Abby watched him push the glass top back into place. She felt a little safer when Angus, with his sharp lizard teeth, was back in the tank.

"Good idea," Mr. Maggioli said. "Yes, absolutely. I'll only be gone for two days, but there's quite a lot for you to remember."

Abby fished around in her backpack for a pencil. "Okay. What's first?"

Mr. Maggioli scratched his nose and considered the question. "Well, let's start with the plants."

"Plants?" echoed Abby, surprised. "I thought you wanted us to take care of Angus."

Mr. Maggioli chuckled. "Yes, that's right.

But maybe you've noticed that Angus doesn't have a water dish. When he's thirsty he licks water off the leaves of the plants. It's very important that you mist the plants every day. Extremely vital."

Abby wrote *mist plants* in her notebook.

"Please use the water in this misting bottle," he said, pointing to a plastic bottle with a pump top. It sat on the shelf above the vivarium beside a box of lightbulbs and other equipment. "Water straight from the tap has chemicals in it that wouldn't be good for Angus. I always let the water sit overnight."

Mr. Maggioli stared at the vivarium for a moment, lost in thought. "What else? Oh yes," he finally said, "the lamp. The heat lamp is on a timer. It comes on in the morning and goes off at night, just like the sun. Actually, it's a combination heat lamp and fluorescent bulb. Angus needs the vitamins the bulb's UV rays provide. Please make sure it's working when you come to feed him."

Abby looked at the flat rock she'd noticed

earlier. "You mean the spotlight?"

Mr. Maggioli nodded. "Yes. It looks like a spotlight, doesn't it? But it's a heat lamp. Angus loves to bask on that rock. Lizards are cold-blooded, as you probably know."

Abby added *check heat lamp* to her list.

"You may have noticed that Angus prefers to be left alone." Mr. Maggioli pulled a tissue from his pocket and dabbed at his wounded finger. "In general, anoles don't like being handled, especially by strangers. Sometimes, if they get really stressed, their tails drop off. In time the tails grow back, but they grow back gray instead of green. So please don't try to pick him up. Don't even try to pet him. He's very quick, and if you're not careful . . ."

Abby glanced at his finger and grimaced. "Don't worry," she said. "We won't touch him."

Mr. Maggioli smiled ruefully. "No, I guess you probably won't. Now, about his meals," he continued. "Angus needs to have his food dusted with vitamin powder every week or so, but I've already taken care of that. His food is over there, in that pail. He also needs a small amount of fruit. I'll leave a plate of orange slices in the refrigerator in the kitchen. Put the plate in the vivarium. Angus will eat what he wants."

Abby wrote down *orange slices*.

"Now, he needs to be fed every day . . ."

Just then the doorbell rang. Mr. Maggioli left to answer it and Abby checked her notes. She added *feed daily* to her list. So far, this job looked like a piece of cake. Even if Angus was a little temperamental.

"This will be easy," she whispered to Tess. "Don't you think?"

5 Whir, Buzz, Thump

Tess inched away from the vivarium. She growled softly.

"Oh, come on," said Abby. "Angus isn't that bad. So he bit Mr. Maggioli. We don't need to pick him up. We don't even need to touch him. All we have to do is squirt his plants and feed him." She added quietly, "It's only for two days."

Tess looked uncertain.

"I know we thought we'd be looking after regular pets," Abby said. "Pets with fur. But this is our first pet-sitting job together and I know we can do it. You still want to be my helper, don't you?"

Tess nodded bravely. She took a step toward the vivarium. Angus lay on his branch, still as a statue. He was brown again, but they knew how to spot him now. He stared through the glass at them, unblinking.

"See?" Abby said. "He's just a harmless little lizard. Nothing to be scared of."

"Okay," Tess whispered. She leaned forward to get a better look.

Angus was stretched out on his branch, as usual. Then, without warning, he was on his feet, glaring at Tess. A reddish-colored flap of skin fanned open under his throat. Another flap sprang up on the back of his neck. He didn't utter a sound, but both Abby and Tess jumped back as though they'd been zapped by electricity.

Tess yelped and ran behind the desk. She disappeared into the small space between the drawers.

Abby's heart thudded wildly in her chest. She could hear Tess whimpering. She wanted to run after her to tell her it was okay, but she couldn't tear her eyes away from Angus. He danced along his branch, the strange flaps of skin billowing like sails in the wind.

"Angus! What are you doing?" It was Mr. Maggioli. He walked quickly to where Abby stood and said apologetically, "I'm sorry, did he frighten you?"

Abby gulped. "No," she lied.

He gave her a comforting pat on the shoulder. "Don't worry," he said. "Angus won't hurt you. He's just showing his dewlap and his dorsal crest. It's something green anoles do when they're excited or upset." He stopped and looked around the room. "Where's Tess?"

A frightened wail floated up from under the desk.

"Uh, Angus kind of startled Tess," Abby explained. She knew from experience that Tess wouldn't budge until she was good and ready. "She'll be fine."

Mr. Maggioli eyed the desk doubtfully. "Are you sure? Should we call your mother?"

"Don't worry," Abby assured him. "Just give her a minute to calm down."

"Well, if you're certain," he said. He gave the desk one last look. "Where was I before we were interrupted?"

Abby checked her notes. "You were telling me about his food."

"Oh, yes," he said, his face brightening. "Of course. Well, in addition to spraying the

plants with water and giving him orange slices, Angus needs to be fed once a day. I keep his regular food in this pail."

Mr. Maggioli motioned to the pail he'd shown Abby earlier. Actually, it was a trash can, like the kind people put outside on garbage day. But this one had an unusual lid. The center had been cut out and replaced by a piece of screen, creating a window. Abby got a weird feeling in the pit of her stomach. Was it her imagination, or did the pail seem to be making an odd noise?

Mr. Maggioli picked up a smaller pail sitting nearby. "This is my own special recipe. It's a mixture of cat food, alfalfa pellets and calcium. Feed it to them once a day, otherwise they'll get hungry and eat each other."

Abby was confused. "Them?"

Mr. Maggioli raised his eyebrows. "Yes, I assumed you knew. All lizards eat a diet that consists mainly of live insects. Spiders, tiny earthworms, flies. But there's one insect they like best of all."

Abby felt sick. Did he just say insects? Live insects? The noise Abby thought she heard earlier seemed louder now. *Whir, buzz, thump. Whir, buzz, thump.*

Holding her breath, she forced herself to walk over to the pail. She peered through the screen. It took a moment for her eyes to adjust to the dim light inside, but then she saw what was making all the noise.

"Crickets," Abby gulped.

6 No Turning Back

Abby sat cross-legged on her bed, still in her windbreaker, paging through a book on reptiles. "Come see this, Tess," she said. "Green anoles are actually pretty cool."

Usually Tess loved to read with Abby. But this time she didn't move. She sat on her bed on the other side of the room, playing a game of cards. The game didn't seem to have any rules, but neither Tess nor the scruffy brown monkey she was playing against cared. She shook her head at Abby and growled softly.

"Oh come on," said Abby. "Angus wasn't that bad. I thought he was kind of cute, didn't you? I mean, until he . . ."

Tess growled again.

Abby sighed. "Yeah, I know. Until he bit Mr. Maggioli. And did that weird thing with his skin." She shivered slightly at the memory. "But it says here that green anoles are nonconfrontational. That means they don't like to fight."

Tess said nothing. She dealt another hand of cards to her monkey, Boo Boo. He'd been around forever. His fur was matted from hundreds of trips through the washing machine and he'd lost his tail years ago. But Tess didn't care. None of her other animals loved her as much as Boo Boo did.

Abby flipped ahead a few pages. "Look at this. Anoles were the first lizards to be sold as pets. Ladies used to wear them as lapel pins. They put tiny collars on them and chained them to their shirts. Don't you think that's horrible? Those poor little anoles."

Tess scooped the cards into an untidy pile. Then she tried to shuffle them. Cards flew across the bed. She didn't care about anoles.

Abby gave up. She snapped the thick book shut and tossed it on the end of her bed. "Okay. I understand. But you're going to help me, right? You can't just pick the jobs you like."

Tess snorted. "I'm not feeding him crickets."

Abby rubbed her temples like Mom did

when she'd been painting too long. Tess could be so stubborn. "Fine," she said finally. "I'll feed him the crickets myself. But you're going to help with the rest, aren't you?"

"No crickets," repeated Tess firmly.

"Forget about the crickets," cried Abby. She jumped off the bed and glared at Tess, her fists on her hips. If she had to hear one more word about crickets . . . .

Something small and hard hit the floor and rolled across the carpet. Tess looked at it and pounced. Before Abby could say a word, Tess had the object between her teeth. She shook her head back and forth furiously, then spat it out.

"What's that?" she asked, looking up at Abby. She sniffed the brightly colored tube. "Lipstick?"

"Give it back, Tess," said Abby. "Right now."

"It smells yummy." Tess studied the lettering on the tube. She was just learning how to read. She tried sounding out the words.

"Ta . . . tan . . . what does it say?"

Abby snatched it from the floor. "Tantalizing Tangerine. And no, it's not lipstick. You know I'm not allowed to wear makeup. It's lip gloss. Which is completely different. And it's not even mine, so I'll thank you not to chew on it."

Tess cocked her head to one side. "It looks like lipstick to me."

"Well it's not," Abby said. She wiped the tube on her pants.

"Whose is it?"

Abby inspected the tube for damage, then tucked it away in a cubbyhole in her desk. "It's Rachel's. She dropped it in the schoolyard when she was running to catch the bus. I picked it up and brought it home. I'll give it to her on Monday." She gave Tess her most serious look. "Don't even think about touching it."

Tess climbed onto her bed and began gathering up the cards. "Why would I want to touch your dumb makeup anyway?" she said with a shrug.

Abby shot her a look of disbelief. "Oh, come on, Tess. You always get into my stuff."

Tess ignored her and dealt the cards. "One for Boo Boo, three for me," she said to herself. "One for Boo Boo, five for me. One for Boo Boo . . ."

"Do you think that just because we share a bedroom you can touch everything?" asked Abby. She was starting to get irritated. "What's mine is mine, you know. It's off limits."

Tess kept on dealing. "I don't touch your stuff."

Abby pointed at Boo Boo. "Oh yeah? That looks like my belt."

"That's not a belt," giggled Tess. "That's Boo Boo's leash."

Abby marched over to the bed, grabbed Tess's monkey and undid the belt from around its neck. "It's my belt."

Tess stared at her. She snatched Boo Boo out of Abby's hands and clutched him tightly to her chest. "Why are you being so mean?"

Abby didn't know what to say. She

couldn't think why she was so upset. She didn't really care about the belt. She didn't even wear it anymore. Maybe it was the pet-sitting job. And Angus. She hated to admit it, but she was a bit scared of him. And no matter what she said to Tess, she didn't know how she was going to make herself reach into that bucket of crickets when it was time to feed him tomorrow.

Tess got to whimper and whine when she was scared of something, but Abby had to be grown-up and mature. She'd convinced her parents she was responsible enough to pet-sit. And she was. She just wished Angus was something else, like a kitten.

Abby straightened her shoulders. She could do this. She could handle a few crickets. They were only bugs, after all. Mr. Maggioli had shown her how to use a net to scoop up two or three at a time. Then all she had to do was release them into the vivarium. Angus would do the rest.

It was simple, really. Without a word, she

left the room. She was tired of thinking about Angus. She needed to do something to take her mind off lizards and crickets. Maybe she'd go watch a little TV.

Anything but the nature channel.

7 Don't Forget Angus

Abby wrapped her blankets more tightly around her head, but it was useless. She could still hear the noise. Tess was doing something over on her side of the bedroom, something very, very loud. *Squeak, squeak, thud! Squeak, squeak, thud!*

Abby put her wrist close to her face and pressed the shiny knob on the side of her watch. The face glowed green under the covers. 6:48 a.m. She groaned. Usually Tess didn't wake up this early.

Squeak, squeak, THUD!

Abby jerked upright and clawed the blankets off her face. "What are you doing, Tess?" she cried.

"It's Saturday," announced Tess. Smiling happily, she bounced up and down on her bed. *Squeak, squeak, squeak.*

Abby rubbed her eyes. They felt gritty and tired. "I know what day it is," she said. "What I don't understand is why you're making so much noise this early in the morning."

"Sleep is boring," giggled Tess. The mattress squeaked louder the higher she bounced. She threw herself off the bed and landed with a thud on the floor. Then she dropped down on all fours and scrambled across the carpet to Abby's desk.

"Hey," protested Abby. Her desk was private. Completely off limits. Tess knew that. But she disappeared under the desk anyway.

The desk swayed back and forth as though the house was being rocked by an earthquake. A cup full of pens and pencils tipped over and spilled its contents. A bottle of sparkle nail polish clattered across the surface of the desk and fell over the edge. A small dish of change, mostly pennies, dropped to the floor and the coins scattered everywhere.

"Hey," Abby cried again. She flung back the covers and jumped to her feet. "My stuff!"

Tess emerged from under the desk with a battered rubber bone clenched between her

teeth. It was her favorite chew toy. Still on her hands and knees, she gave a muffled bark and scampered to her side of the room. She leapt onto her bed and spat the bone out on her pillow. Then she stared at Abby, panting eagerly.

Abby had to smile. Most little kids had a favorite toy, usually a stuffed animal or something soft and cuddly. But not Tess. She had an oversized rubber bone.

Abby shook her head and bent to retrieve the nail polish. She was the one who had bought the bone for Tess in the first place, so she really shouldn't complain. And it had come in handy. Tess had lost her first baby tooth while gnawing on it.

"Why did you have to get up so early today?" she complained mildly. "It's not even seven o'clock yet."

Tess cocked her head and peered sideways at Abby. "What about Angus?"

Angus.

Abby had forgotten all about him. Today was their first day on the job. Mr. Maggioli was gone on his trip and Angus was waiting to be fed. Suddenly she didn't feel the least bit sleepy. She shoved her feet into her slippers, tugged on her housecoat and headed for the kitchen.

"C'mon," she called. "Let's have breakfast. Then we'll head over to Mr. Maggioli's house."

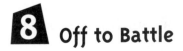

8 Off to Battle

Dad sat at the table, sipping orange juice and scanning the newspaper. "Good morning, girls," he greeted them cheerfully as they burst into the kitchen.

Abby gave him a kiss on the forehead. "Morning."

"Woof," said Tess. She threw her arms around his neck and snuffled his cheek.

"Feel like some of my famous purple-polka-dot pancakes?" he asked with a grin. For Dad, Saturday mornings meant whipping up a big batch of blueberry pancakes. Usually Abby enjoyed helping him, but this morning she was in too much of a hurry.

"No thanks, Dad." She popped two slices of thick brown bread into the toaster. She found the marmalade and the jar of peanut butter and helped herself to some orange juice. "We're kind of in a rush. Where's Mom?"

"She was up late working on a painting,"

Dad answered, his attention on the newspaper. "She's still sleeping."

"At least someone in this house gets to sleep in," Abby muttered. But she didn't really mean it. Now that Tess had reminded her about Angus, she was eager to get on with the day.

"Eat faster, Tess," she said. A blob of marmalade clung to the corner of her mouth and she licked it off impatiently. "We've got to get going."

"Where are you headed so early?" Dad looked up from the comics.

"We've got a pet-sitting job today," she said, chewing quickly as she talked. "We're taking care of Mr. Maggioli's lizard."

"Awful Angus," growled Tess.

Abby rolled her eyes. "He's not awful," she said. "He's just a harmless little lizard."

"Did he leave you the key to his house?" Dad asked, concerned. "Do you need a ride?"

Abby shoved the last bite of toast into her mouth. "Nope and nope," she said. "He left the key under a flowerpot and it's not far so we'll walk. Mom knows all about it."

Dad appeared satisfied with this. He went back to his paper. "Okay, then. Have fun."

The grass was still wet with dew as Abby and Tess found their way back to Mr. Maggioli's yellow house. Abby zipped up her windbreaker and shivered a little. It was still chilly in the mornings, although by afternoon the sun would be warm and bright. She could tell that summer was just around the corner.

Abby pulled her notebook out of her pocket. She studied her notes as they walked along, although she didn't really need to. She was sure she knew exactly what to do today. Squirt the plants, put the orange slices in the vivarium, feed Angus a couple of crickets. She shuddered and stuffed the notebook back into her pocket. No problem. She could handle it.

The key was hidden exactly where Mr. Maggioli had said it would be. Abby tipped up the heavy flowerpot and Tess fished it out. The house seemed too quiet when they let themselves in.

Abby tiptoed down the hallway, past the

paintings of bananas and grapes and pineapples. Tess was right behind her. They stopped in the kitchen to get the orange slices from the fridge. Next stop, the study. And Angus.

"Why don't you give him the oranges," Abby suggested. She glanced sideways at the cricket pail, then quickly looked away. "I'll mist the plants."

Tess accepted the plate of oranges. She took a few steps toward the vivarium, then hesitated. Abby brushed past Tess. She'd show her there was nothing to be afraid of.

It was easy to spot Angus today. He lay sprawled on the sunning rock, basking in the warm circle of light. Abby tried to push the glass top to one side. Nothing happened. She tried again but her fingers slipped. It was heavier than it looked.

"Give me a hand, Tess," she said.

Tess came a few steps closer, then stopped again. She frowned and stared through the glass. Angus remained motionless on his sunning rock.

"Come on," Abby urged her sister. "I need your help."

Tess blinked. She set the oranges down on the desk and together she and Abby managed to shift the heavy lid sideways. Angus didn't move a muscle.

"See," Abby said. She pointed at the lazy lizard. "He's not going to do anything. He'll probably just lie there the whole time."

Tess didn't look convinced.

Abby picked up the spray bottle and checked the nozzle to be sure the water would come out in a fine mist. She was careful to give each plant several good squirts, paying close attention to the one with spiky leaves in the corner. She took much longer than necessary. After a few minutes every plant was dripping wet and she knew she couldn't put it off any longer.

It was time to face the crickets.

9 Who's Watching Who?

"Keep an eye on Angus," Abby told Tess. She took a deep breath and went over to where the pails were.

The smaller pail of cricket food rattled softly when Abby picked it up. She pried the lid off and filled the small scoop inside with the crumbly mixture. It didn't look so bad. Kind of like chunky granola. She glanced at the cricket pail. Now came the hard part.

Whir. Buzz. Thump.

Reluctantly, Abby walked toward the noise. It grew louder as she got closer. Abby shivered. She supposed the whirs and buzzes and thumps were a good thing since they meant the crickets were still alive. And probably hungry. She hoped they hadn't started snacking on each other.

She knew Tess was watching so she tried not to look nervous. Holding the scoop of cricket chow in one hand, Abby peered cautiously through the screen. At the bottom of the pail, over to one side, sat a long, shallow ceramic dish filled with soggy cotton. Mr. Maggioli had explained that this was the crickets' drinking water. The cotton soaked up the water so the crickets could drink it without drowning.

The other side of the pail held egg cartons stacked one on top of the other like a crazy cardboard apartment building. Scattered here and there were toilet paper tubes for the crickets to hide and sleep in. On top of the egg cartons was a plastic food container that looked like it had once held yogurt or cottage cheese.

But that wasn't all that was in the pail. There were crickets too. Dozens and dozens of crickets. They hopped among the egg cartons and clustered around the drinking dish.

Abby tried not to let her hand shake as she opened the lid. The minute she touched it the crickets froze. She was certain they were staring at her. The lid lifted easily. Abby was so intent on what she was doing, she barely noticed Tess creep up behind her.

Abby poured the cricket food into the plastic container and quickly dropped the lid back into place. So far so good. She set the scoop down on the floor and picked up the long-handled net Mr. Maggioli had shown her yesterday. The netting was fine and deep.

Lifting the lid up again, but not too high, Abby lowered the net into the pail. She heard Tess right behind her, whining softly, but she couldn't think about Tess now.

A group of large crickets sat near the edge of an egg carton. Carefully, Abby steered the net toward them. Two crickets jumped out of the way. That left three. Abby bit her lip and eased the net closer. Then, in one swift movement, she scooped them up and flicked her wrist. The crickets tumbled into the folds of the net.

"Gotcha," she whispered.

At first the crickets lay still. Then they began to struggle, their legs kicking wildly. Abby felt that strange sensation bubble up in the pit of her stomach again.

She eased the net out of the pail and replaced the cover carefully. The last thing she wanted was a prison break. She could just imagine coming back tomorrow and finding the house overrun with crickets. Satisfied that they couldn't escape, she turned toward the vivarium with her net of squirming insects.

Tess yelped and jumped out of her path. Abby ignored her. Every ounce of her concentration was focused on keeping the crickets in the net. She could hardly bear to look at them. She didn't like bugs. They were ugly and bothersome and just plain gross. She certainly never collected them or played with them like some of the kids at school. Even so, she felt sorry for the crickets in her net. And just a tiny bit guilty. She was, after all, delivering them to Angus for his breakfast.

"Sorry guys," she said. "I don't really want to do this."

She carried them to the vivarium. Tess followed a few steps behind. The glass lid was still pushed to one side and all Abby had to do was lower the net into the tank and shake the crickets loose. The rest was up to Angus.

Suddenly Abby froze. That queasy, uneasy feeling was back. Something had happened, she just knew it. She was almost afraid to look in the vivarium.

If Tess had been watching her feed and capture the crickets, who had been watching Angus?

10 A Million Hiding Places

Angus was gone.

Frantically, Abby searched the vivarium. The rock was bare. The branch was empty. She looked behind every log and leaf, but there was no sign of Angus.

"Tess," she wailed. "I told you to keep an eye on him!"

Tess whimpered. Abby opened her mouth to shout, then snapped it shut again. She'd have to get mad at Tess later. Right now she had to find Angus, and fast.

Maybe he hadn't gone too far. She turned in a circle, taking in the bookshelves and the untidy stacks of papers. No lizard. Angus could be just about anywhere. She froze when she noticed the windows. Were they open? With a sinking feeling she scanned one, then the other. They were shut tight, thank goodness. At least he wasn't outside.

"Quick, Tess," she cried, thinking fast.

"Close the door. We have to trap him in this room!"

But Tess was rooted to the spot. Her eyes filled with tears and her quiet whimpering grew louder. She stared at Abby, too frightened to move.

Abby ran past her to the door and slammed it shut. Tess was proving to be absolutely useless as a helper.

She tried to think logically. With the windows and door shut, he couldn't get out of the room. Mr. Maggioli had told them Angus was good at hiding. So all they had to do was find him. And catch him. And somehow get him safely back in the vivarium without getting bitten.

Abby swallowed nervously. She needed a plan. "Let's split up," she said to Tess. "You look on that side of the room and I'll look over here. Okay?"

Tess stopped whimpering, but she didn't answer.

"Come on, Tess," she pleaded. "We have to find him. I really need your help."

Tess shook her head. Her eyes were wide with fear.

Abby tried again. "Look, I know you're scared," she said with forced calm. "Just help me find him. That's all. I'll do the rest."

A small movement caught Abby's attention. She looked down and realized she was still holding the net with the three doomed crickets. The sight of the net gave her an idea. It had a long handle. If she used it to scoop up Angus, he couldn't get near enough to bite her. But first she needed to get rid of the crickets.

She glanced at the cricket pail and then at the vivarium. No matter how long it took, she had to find Angus, and when she did he'd still need to be fed. Why not dump the crickets in the vivarium now?

She held the net upside down in the glass tank and shook it. The crickets struggled free and darted into the plants. But without the lid in place, they could easily escape.

Abby rubbed her right temple and tried to think. If she closed the heavy lid now the crickets wouldn't be able to get out. But then she'd have to struggle with it again if she caught Angus. When she caught Angus, she corrected herself. What she needed was something to keep the crickets trapped in the tank. Something light that would be easy to remove in a hurry.

She wiped a bead of sweat off her forehead. Maybe it was because the door was shut, or maybe it was because she was frightened, but all of a sudden she felt unbearably hot. With one eye on the crickets, she unzipped her windbreaker and shrugged out of it. She held it for a moment, thinking. The thin material felt smooth and light in her hand.

She had an idea. She shook open the jacket and draped it over the opening. It fit perfectly. The empty sleeves hung down the sides of the glass, giving the vivarium a limp hug. It wasn't much, but it would keep the crickets in. For awhile, anyway.

That problem solved, Abby turned back to the room. Now she had to find Angus. She

had a feeling this was easier said than done. The plate of orange slices sat untouched on the desk. Abby snatched it up. She peeled off the plastic wrap and tossed it aside. She'd use the scent of the fruit to lure Angus out of hiding!

"He can't have gone far," she said with determination. "I'll start near the vivarium and work my way out."

That's exactly what she did. She got down on her hands and knees and searched the floor inch by inch. She remembered how Mr. Maggioli had spoken gently to Angus to calm him down.

"Here Angus," she crooned. She held the orange slices low to the floor. "Come on boy, I've got a treat for you."

Abby worked slowly and carefully. She bumped into Tess, who still refused to move.

Ignoring her, she continued until she reached the door.

No Angus.

I'm not giving up, Abby thought to herself. She checked inside a porcelain vase and behind a bronze statue of a horse. She pulled the heavy drapes away from the walls and shook them gingerly. Tentatively, she poked her head under the big wooden desk.

Still no Angus.

Abby refused to give up. She was determined not to go home until Angus was found and safely returned to captivity. There were a million hiding places in this room, but she just had to find him. Even if it meant searching all day.

11 Awful, Awful Angus

One by one, Abby pulled the dusty books off their shelves to peer behind them. She shifted the plate of orange slices to her left hand so she could work faster. Mr. Maggioli had a vast collection of books. She wondered if she really would be here all day.

It would go a lot faster, Abby thought angrily, if Tess would help.

"Woof!" barked Tess suddenly. The unexpected noise startled Abby and the plate of oranges crashed to the floor. Tess barked again and again, loud and furious.

"Are you crazy?" cried Abby. "He'll never come out if you scare him. Stop it Tess!"

But Tess didn't stop. Her frantic barking bounced off the walls and filled the room. She tilted her head back sharply and began to howl at the ceiling.

"Tess!" yelled Abby. "Knock it off!"

Surprisingly, she did. The room became

dead quiet. But Tess continued to point her nose at the ceiling. She reminded Abby of one of those hunting dogs. The kind that pointed out game for their masters . . . .

Abby threw her own head back. Sure enough, clinging to the lamp above Tess was a slim green lizard. The flaps of skin on his neck and under his chin flared silently.

"Angus," she cried. Relief flooded through her. They'd found him! Well, Tess had found him, but she'd think about that later. Right now she had to capture the runaway lizard.

But how?

She eyed the lamp, which dangled a few feet below the ceiling. The handle on the cricket net was long, but nowhere near long enough to reach Angus. Maybe if she stood on something . . . .

The desk. If she stood on tiptoe on Mr. Maggioli's desk and stretched her arm out as far as possible, she just might be able to get him. It was worth a try. As quietly as she could, she climbed onto the polished desktop. She inhaled slowly and raised the net.

"Please don't move," she whispered anxiously. If she spooked Angus he might skitter away and she'd be right back where she started. Even worse, he might lose his footing and fall on her head!

She didn't have to worry. Angus and Tess were locked in a serious staring battle. Tess glared at the lizard and let out a long, low growl. Angus glowered at Tess and displayed his dewlap and dorsal crest threateningly. Neither one paid any attention to Abby.

Abby shuffled across the slippery surface of the desk. Holding the very end of the handle, she lifted the net toward Angus. It almost reached his tail. Keeping it steady, she inched forward a bit more. Her toes were nearly at the edge of the desk. She teetered for a moment, then caught her balance. She stretched her arm out as far as it could go. Just a little further . . . .

With a smooth flick of her wrist, Abby knocked the lizard into the net. She had him! She pinched the top of the net shut, trapping him for good. She wasn't taking any chances. There was no way she was going to let Angus escape again.

Tess ran to the vivarium and jerked Abby's windbreaker free. Abby dropped Angus into the tank, net and all. Together, Abby and Tess pushed the glass lid into place.

Abby's shoulders sagged with relief. Angus was safe once again.

The orange slices lay scattered on the floor. Luckily, the plate wasn't broken. Abby slowly gathered everything up. Angus had missed his fruit snack today, but she didn't care. He'd just have to wait until tomorrow because there was no way she was opening the tank again.

"Come on, Tess," she said in a tired voice. "Let's go home."

Angus stared at Tess through the glass.

"Awful, awful Angus," muttered Tess.

This time, Abby had to agree.

The next morning Abby dawdled over breakfast. She took her time deciding what to wear. She brushed her teeth and washed her face as slowly as possible.

She was trying to decide whether to pull her hair back with clips or wear it in a pony-tail when there was a knock on the bath-room door.

"What?" she called.

The door opened and Tess peeked in. "Are you done yet?"

"Almost." Abby caught her sister's eye in the mirror. "Are you coming with me today?"

she asked. It wouldn't surprise her a bit if Tess didn't want to see Angus again. She wasn't sure she wanted to either.

Tess nodded. "Yup."

Abby raised her eyebrows. "Really? Even after yesterday?"

"I'm not scared," Tess said defiantly. She hesitated, then asked in a small voice, "Don't you want me to come?"

"Sure I do," said Abby. She decided on the purple clips and fastened them securely in her hair. "He doesn't scare me either," she added, though she wasn't being one hundred percent truthful.

Tess tried to smile.

"Don't worry," Abby reassured her. "It's our last day. There's no way Angus will escape again."

Finally Abby couldn't put it off any longer. It was time to go see Angus. Low clouds threatened rain this morning, she'd heard the radio announce. She grabbed her windbreaker from the front closet. Tess put on her raincoat.

"How come you decided to come today?" she asked Tess as they walked along the cracked cement sidewalk. "I didn't think you'd ever go back there."

Tess smiled shyly. "I like being your helper."

Abby had been angry with Tess when Angus escaped. Absolutely furious, to be honest. But Tess had been the one to find Angus. If she hadn't spotted him on the lamp, they might still be there, searching.

Abby smiled back, "Yeah, me too."

They got the key from under the flowerpot and opened the front door.

"You get the fruit this time," Abby said. "I'll do the rest."

Tess nodded and padded off toward the kitchen. Abby headed to the back of the house. The air in the study was as stale as old socks. She glanced at the windows. Forget it. Those windows were staying shut, even though Angus was safely locked up.

Abby went over to the cricket pail first. She measured out a scoop of dried food and fed the crickets, careful not to let any jump free. She used the spray bottle to moisten their cotton. Finally, it was time to feed Angus his lunch. But where was the net?

Tess came up beside her, holding the plate of oranges. "Got them," she said.

"Good," Abby replied absently. She looked behind the table and on the floor. "Do you see the net anywhere? It was here yesterday, but I can't find it."

Tess wrinkled her nose. "He's got it."

Abby didn't understand. "Huh?"

"Awful Angus."

"What are you talking about?" Abby asked. Then she remembered. Yesterday she'd dropped Angus, and the net, into the tank.

"Oh, right." She looked across the room and sighed. She couldn't put it off forever. It was time to say hello to Angus.

The heat lamp glowed yellow in the vivarium. She half expected to find Angus missing, but she spotted his tail sticking out from behind a rock. The cricket net lay on its side, its fine mesh caught on the plant with the spiky leaves. Whew. Everything was perfectly normal. Just the way she liked it.

Abby ran through the checklist in her mind. She decided to squirt the plants first, although she could still see beads of moisture clinging to some of the leaves. When the plants were wet she'd give Angus the orange slices. After missing yesterday's snack, he was probably waiting for them.

"Come help me with the lid," she called to Tess, who was still standing by the crickets.

Tess hesitated for a moment. Then she set the plate of oranges on Mr. Maggioli's desk and joined her sister.

Abby wiped her hands on her jeans and gripped the heavy lid. "Grab the other end," she told Tess.

Tess took a step, then stopped. Abby sighed. Not this again. "Come on, Tess," she said, keeping her voice calm. "I need you."

But Tess wouldn't come any closer. Instead, she backed away slowly, her eyes fixed on the vivarium. She growled deep in her throat.

"What's wrong?" asked Abby. She followed her sister's gaze.

Angus had stepped out into the open. Abby watched as he carefully picked his way up the climbing branch, his skinny green legs lifting delicately with each step. He seemed okay. His skin flaps weren't even flaring.

Then he smiled.

Well, maybe it wasn't an actual smile, but his thin lizard lips parted in what appeared to be a wide, wet grin. A glossy orange ring circled his mouth. It reminded Abby of sloppy clown make-up. Abby stared at him in disbelief. It almost looked like Angus was wearing . . . .

"Lipstick," yelped Tess.

The sunning rock caught Abby's eye. She gasped. A pool of orange goo shimmered in the center of the rock. Orange streaks showed where the liquid had oozed down the sides and soaked into the sand below. Abby noticed sticky lizard footprints leading away from the rock.

And there, right beside the telltale footprints, lay a tube of Tantalizing Tangerine lip gloss.

13 From Bad to Worse

"Rachel's lip gloss!" exclaimed Abby. "How did that get in there?"

Tess looked baffled. "I don't . . ."

"I can't believe you did this, Tess," cried Abby. She blinked back the tears that threatened to spill. "You're always getting into my stuff! You have no respect for my privacy at all! But this time you really messed up. Because that," Abby continued, pointing at the tube, "isn't even mine. How could you do this?"

"But I . . ."

Abby didn't wait for an explanation. "You're supposed to be my helper, Tess. And a helper is supposed to share the work. Not wreck things. You haven't been any help to me at all!"

Abby paused, her breath catching in her throat. She waited for Tess to say something. Tess stared at her. After a moment she turned and ran from the room. The front door slammed and Abby knew she was gone.

For a split second Abby considered running after her, but she didn't. She was too fed up. She couldn't leave now anyway because Angus still needed to be fed. Plus there was that disgusting mess to clean up.

Abby looked at the sunning rock and felt a knot of anger in her chest. Why did Tess always do these things? The kid was a walking disaster. She was no good at helping. In fact, she had even let Angus escape. The more Abby thought about it, the angrier she became.

All she wanted to do right now was go home, but she couldn't. She had to be responsible. The glass lid was heavy, but she managed to move it. Angus took one look at her and disappeared behind a fern. Abby lifted the sticky sunning rock out of the vivarium and set it beside the plate of oranges on the desk.

"I'd better give you these," she muttered, putting the plate in the tank. She grabbed the lip gloss tube and examined it. The cap was loose. She looked inside. Empty.

Feeling angry again, she shoved the tube

in her pocket. Then she closed the vivarium lid with a single hard push.

Clutching the slimy rock in both hands, Abby headed for the kitchen. She placed the rock carefully in the sink, then searched the cupboard below for a sponge and some soap. Luckily, the makeup came off easily.

She washed the tube too. Rachel probably wouldn't want it, especially after a lizard had played with it. But Abby felt bad throwing it out. Better keep it, she thought, sticking it in her pocket. Then she wiped out the sink and headed back to the study with the clean rock.

Being angry at Tess somehow made it easier to feed Angus his lunch. She was too furious to feel nervous. Leaving the rock on the table, she retrieved the net and quickly trapped two crickets. It wasn't easy opening the glass lid with the net in her hand, but she managed it. She shook the crickets loose and watched them run for cover.

Next, Abby dropped the rock into place with a thud. "Oh no," she groaned out loud, noticing the spots of lip gloss on the sand. Frowning, she scratched at the sand until the goo was hidden. She made Angus's tiny lizard tracks disappear too.

When she was done there was no sign that anything unusual had happened. Except, of course, for the evidence that decorated Angus's face. Angus had climbed up on his branch and was watching Abby, his glossy lips pressed shut.

Abby stared at the lizard. "You didn't eat any of that stuff, did you?" she asked suddenly.

What if the ingredients in the lip gloss were toxic? Maybe it smelled like fruit, but it wasn't meant to be eaten. Abby gulped. Angus might be poisoned. He might even die!

Anxiously, she fumbled in her pocket and pulled out the tube. She looked for the list of ingredients. Some of the lettering had been rubbed off, but she could just make out the word Nontoxic. Her shoulders sagged with relief.

There was still the problem of Angus's face. She really should clean it. But how? A lizard wouldn't let you wipe its mouth, like a little kid would. Lizards were unpredictable and had sharp teeth.

Abby thought of Mr. Maggioli's finger and made up her mind. Angus could keep his slick smile. Anyway, the goo would probably come off when he was eating or drinking. One thing was for sure, she wasn't going to risk getting bitten.

Abby checked the room one last time. The lid was on the cricket pail, Angus was fed and the glass top on the vivarium was shut tight. She locked the front door and managed to slip the key into its place under the flowerpot.

Boy, was she glad this job was over. It hadn't been anything like she'd expected. Angus certainly wasn't the kind of pet she'd imagined looking after when they'd hung up their pet-sitting poster a week ago.

They. Her and Tess.

Abby shoved her hands into her pockets and started to walk. Her right hand fingered the empty lip gloss tube. What was she going to say to Tess when she got home? It was true that Tess was much younger. She was less reliable and more forgetful and more easily frightened. Abby understood that Tess didn't like Angus. She could forgive that. But the lip gloss? That was private property.

How many times had she told Tess to leave her stuff alone? And how many times had she found Tess using her favorite things? Like decorating Boo Boo's ears with her new butterfly clips. Enough was enough. Tess had to learn to respect her privacy.

14 A Tough Decision

Abby let herself into the apartment. Two small, dirty running shoes lay scattered by the door. She paused in the front hall to listen. The living room was quiet, which meant Tess wasn't watching TV.

Abby hung her jacket in the closet and walked down the hallway. The door to the bedroom she shared with Tess was shut. That was fine with her. She didn't feel like seeing Tess just yet.

The studio door was shut too. Abby knocked. "Mom," she called, poking her head inside. "Are you busy?"

Mom was standing in front of a large wooden easel. A long thin brush was in one hand and a palette holding dabs of paint was in the other. As usual, she wore an old T-shirt that hung to her knees. She turned to Abby with a welcoming smile.

"Come on in, honey. Tell me what you think."

Abby studied the canvas that rested on the easel. It showed two girls crouched in a field of tall grass and wildflowers. Their faces were hidden by tangled curls. The girls sat with their heads together, gazing at something. For some reason the picture made Abby feel sad.

"It's pretty," she offered. The girls in the painting seemed so happy together. They looked like sisters. Abby bet they didn't have the problems she and Tess had.

"Thanks," Mom said. She sat down on a stool and examined her work. "It's not quite finished yet. How's Angus?"

Abby hadn't told her parents about Angus's escape from the vivarium. She still felt like she had to prove that she was old enough to pet-sit. She didn't want Mom and Dad to think she wasn't responsible.

For a moment, though, she was tempted to tell Mom the whole story. Not just about Angus, but about the crickets and Tess and the lip gloss and everything.

"He's okay," she said instead.

"That's good. When will Mr. Maggioli be back?"

"Tomorrow," said Abby, silently adding, thank goodness.

"I noticed Tess came home by herself today," Mom said casually. She continued to study her painting, but Abby knew she was waiting for an answer. Abby stared at the painting too.

"We had a fight," she admitted finally. "Tess took something from my desk and ruined it. She's always getting into my stuff. I don't think we can pet-sit together anymore."

"That sounds serious," Mom said, dipping her brush into a circle of yellow paint. With one brush stroke she added a glint of sunshine to a blade of grass. "Did Tess say why she did it?"

Abby cleared her throat. She hadn't really given Tess a chance to explain. "Well, no . . ."

Mom dabbed at the canvas, adding highlights to the younger girl's hair. The curls looked so real, Abby felt like she could reach out and touch them.

"Maybe you should talk to her," Mom said gently. "I'm sure Tess wouldn't harm something of yours on purpose. She's very proud to be your partner, you know. She looks up to you, Abby."

"Yeah, sure," said Abby. But she didn't think there was anything Tess could say that would change her mind. Tess stole Rachel's lip gloss and gave it to Angus. It was as simple as that. Why she did it, Abby couldn't guess. But one thing was clear. Having Tess as a helper just wasn't working out.

Maybe it was time to make a new poster.

15 Rachel Has Some Doubts

During supper, Mom and Dad talked about work and friends and what new flowers to plant in the garden. Abby and Tess said little. When Tess passed the bowl of mashed potatoes, Abby accepted it silently. When Abby gave the buns to Tess, she did it without looking at her. Dad watched them with raised eyebrows, but didn't comment.

Bedtime was strained. Abby and Tess put on their pajamas without exchanging a word. The only sound in the room was the opera music that floated up through the floor. Abby pulled back her covers and climbed into bed, careful to keep her eyes on her side of the room.

Mom came in and kissed them both goodnight. She hesitated in the doorway before switching off the light and Abby caught the worried expression on her face. Then she left, the door clicking softly behind her.

Abby lay in the dark and stared at nothing. She heard Tess rustle under her covers on the other side of the room. After a few moments Tess's bed squeaked and Abby heard bare feet pad softly across the carpet. Something cool and hard pressed against her cheek.

"Here," Tess whispered near Abby's ear. "This always makes me feel better."

Abby waited until she heard Tess crawl back into bed, then reached out to touch the object. Her fingers quickly recognized the rubber bone. She felt her resolve weaken.

"Tess?" Her voice sounded loud in the dark. "Why did you take the lip gloss?"

"I didn't," answered Tess. There was a stubborn note in her voice.

"Oh, Tess," said Abby, disappointed. How was she supposed to forgive Tess when she wouldn't tell the truth? Abby rolled toward the wall and tried to fall asleep.

The next morning Abby ate and dressed quickly. She slung her backpack over one shoulder and headed out the door behind Tess. It was a strict family rule that the girls walk to school together. But that didn't mean they had to talk.

When they reached the schoolyard Abby spotted Rachel right away. She wondered what she was going to say as she walked toward her. As far as Rachel knew, her lip gloss was lost forever. She had no idea that Abby had rescued it. What would she say when she found out it was destroyed?

"Hi Abby," said Rachel. "Did you have a fun weekend?"

Abby shook her head. "Not really," she said. "I've got something to tell you, and I don't think you're going to like it."

Rachel gave her a puzzled smile. "Really? What?"

Abby took a deep breath. "Well, remember your lip gloss? The one you brought to school on Friday?"

Rachel nodded sadly. "Yeah. I lost it. It was brand new, too."

"You didn't lose it," Abby said. "You dropped it when you were running for the bus. I

found it and took it home for you."

Rachel's face lit up. "Really? That's great! I thought it was gone for good. Where is it?"

"Well," Abby hesitated. This was going to be harder than she thought. "A lizard ate it. Actually, I think he just tasted it, but it was all melted, so . . ."

"A lizard ate it?" Rachel interrupted. She looked skeptical.

"It's true," Abby insisted. "It's all Tess's fault. We were pet-sitting a lizard on the weekend and Tess took your lip gloss and . . ."

"If you lost it, Abby, just say so," said Rachel. "I won't be mad. But don't make stuff up, okay?"

"I'm not making it up!" Abby said. She reached into her windbreaker pocket. "I've got it right here. See for yourself."

She felt around in her pocket, but it was empty. The tube was gone.

Rachel stared hard at Abby. Then she shrugged. "Whatever," she said. She started to walk away.

"But I'm telling the truth," cried Abby. She remembered putting the lip gloss in her pocket at Mr. Maggioli's. It couldn't have just disappeared. She groped in her pocket again. This time, her fingers discovered something that wasn't supposed to be there.

A hole. It was just big enough for a tube of lip gloss to slip through.

16 The Truth Comes Out

"Woof!"

Abby spun around and saw Tess racing across the playground toward her. There was something in her mouth. She barreled past Abby and caught up to Rachel. She pawed the back of her coat to get her attention. Then Tess spat something on the ground at Rachel's feet.

"Hey!" exclaimed Rachel, turning around. "What are you doing?" She looked at Tess, then at the ground.

"Look," Abby said, pointing. "It's your lip gloss. I told you I was telling the truth."

Rachel bent down and picked up the tube. She turned it over and read the broken lettering. "You're right," she said, surprised. "But where did you get it, Tess?"

Tess barked and sat in the grass, panting proudly. Abby explained. "I've got a hole in my pocket. It must have fallen out on the playground. Right Tess?"

Tess nodded.

"Okay, fine," Rachel said. She pulled off the lid and looked inside. "But it's empty. You don't really think I'm going to believe that a lizard ate my lip gloss, do you?"

"Ask her," Abby said, pointing at Tess. "She's the one who gave it to the lizard in the first place."

Tess bristled. "I did not."

Abby sighed. Why wouldn't Tess just admit it? "Then how did Angus get it? I certainly didn't give it to him. I was busy with the crickets, remember?"

Rachel looked confused. "Who's Angus? What crickets?"

Abby ignored her. "It was either you or me, Tess. And I know I didn't do it. So that leaves you. I just don't understand why you did it."

"I didn't do it," cried Tess. "You did!"

Abby stared at her in disbelief. "What?"

Tess nodded vigorously. "I found it in our room, but I'm not supposed to touch your stuff, so I put it back in your coat pocket."

Suddenly, it all began to make sense.

"The lip gloss fell out of my desk when you were chasing your chewy bone," Abby said slowly, thinking out loud. "Later you found it on the floor, but you were scared I'd accuse you of taking it, right?"

"Woof," Tess replied.

"So you stuck it in my pocket," she continued. "It must have fallen out the hole when I used my windbreaker to keep the crickets in the vivarium." Abby felt a pang of guilt. If only she hadn't been so grouchy that day.

"I didn't know the pocket had a hole," Tess said timidly.

Tess had been telling the truth all along. She didn't invade Abby's privacy. She didn't steal the lip gloss and she didn't put it in the vivarium. And Abby hadn't even given her a chance to explain.

"There really is a lizard?" asked Rachel. She looked at the two sisters, trying to make sense of it all.

"Yes," cried Abby and Tess together.

"This is too weird," said Rachel. She glanced down at the tube in her hand. "What am I supposed to do with this?"

"Throw it away," Abby said with a laugh. "We'll buy you a new one, right Tess?"

"Woof, woof," barked Tess happily.

17 A Job Well Done

Abby wasn't eager to see Angus again, but she and Tess had promised to stop by Mr. Maggioli's house after school. She was looking forward to getting paid. She just hoped the lip gloss had worn off by the time Mr. Maggioli got home from his trip.

Ignoring the flowerpot, Abby knocked on the front door.

Mr. Maggioli greeted them warmly. "Hello, girls. Please come in. Angus will be delighted to see you again."

Abby felt hopeful. Mr. Maggioli wouldn't act this friendly if he'd come home to a lizard wearing makeup, would he?

Tess snorted.

Abby spoke quickly to cover her sister's rudeness. "How was your trip?"

"Fine, just fine. It's always good to be home, though," Mr. Maggioli answered, closing the door behind them.

He beamed at the girls. "Thank you for taking such good care of Angus," he said. "I enjoyed my trip so much more knowing he was in good hands. You didn't run into any difficulties, did you?"

Abby and Tess exchanged glances. Was this a trick question? "No, of course not," Abby lied. "Was everything, um, okay when you got home?"

"Oh yes, just wonderful." Mr. Maggioli said. "But I'm sure you want to see Angus." He strode down the hall toward the study. Abby and Tess followed reluctantly. Soon they were standing in front of the vivarium.

"It's snack time," Mr. Maggioli said. He picked up a ripe banana, peeled it and mashed it on a small plate. He opened the vivarium, then hesitated. "Pardon my manners. Perhaps you'd like to feed Angus one last time?"

Tess started to shake her head, but Abby jabbed her in the ribs. "No, you go ahead, Mr. Maggioli," she said. "I think Angus missed you while you were gone."

Mr. Maggioli chuckled. "You know, I do believe you're right about that. I know I missed him terribly." He placed the plate in the tank and stroked Angus with one long, thin finger. "He's such a good pet."

Tess snorted again. This time Abby couldn't think of anything to say to cover it up.

Mr. Maggioli looked at them and laughed. "You must think I'm crazy to be so attached to a lizard," he said. He petted Angus again and asked, "Did I ever tell you why I named him Angus?"

Abby shook her head, embarrassed.

"His name means "unique" in Celtic. Which is exactly what I was looking for in a pet. Something entirely different from the ordinary. People usually keep such boring pets."

He left Angus to his snack and closed the tank. "He suits me perfectly, girls. Angus is definitely unique."

Abby glanced at her sister. Tess grinned and let her tongue loll out the side of her mouth. Abby looked from Tess to the lizard and back to

Tess again. "I understand completely," she said with a smile.

Suddenly Mr. Maggioli clapped his hands. "Now, payment for a job well done," he said.

He pulled open the top drawer of his desk and withdrew an envelope. He handed it to Abby with a flourish, saying, "I shall be sure to call you again if I find myself in need of your services."

Abby tucked the envelope into her backpack. It felt great to be paid. She had all kinds of ideas for what to do with her share of the money. Still, she hoped Mr. Maggioli wasn't planning on taking another trip any time soon. She wasn't sure she was ready to face another weekend with Angus.

"We'll have to use some of the money we earned to buy new lip gloss for Rachel," Abby said to Tess as they walked home.

"Woof," agreed Tess.

The sunshine was bright and Abby lifted her face toward the warm rays. She paused on the sidewalk to take off her windbreaker, then stuffed it in her backpack. "Remind me to fix that hole in my pocket, Tess," she added. "It's caused us enough trouble."

Tess smiled and nodded.

They walked along the sidewalk in companionable silence. Pet-sitting Angus had turned out to be much more difficult than Abby had expected. She wondered what their next job would be like. Whatever it was, she and Tess would handle it together.

"I sure hope the next animal we pet-sit will be a little more normal," she said suddenly. "I'll be glad if I never see another lizard again."

Tess grinned mischievously. "Or another cricket!"

Abby and Tess Pet-Sitters™

Join the Abby and Tess Pet-Sitters™ Club, where you can send electronic animal postcards to your friends, write to "Dear Abby and Tess" about your pet problems, enter the Favorite Pet contest for prizes, become a "published" writer, play games and solve puzzles. Guess the secret password to get inside our tree-house headquarters!

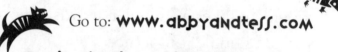

Go to: **www.abbyandtess.com**

Don't miss these other great books in the Abby and Tess Pet-Sitters™ series!

Parrots Don't Make House Calls
1-894222-45-8 available now
$6.95 CDN, $5.95 US

Goats Don't Brush Their Teeth
1-894222-59-8 available now
$6.95 CDN, $5.95 US

Ants Don't Catch Flying Saucers
1-894222-31-8 available now
$6.95 CDN, $5.95 US

Hamsters Don't Glow in the Dark
1-894222-15-6 available now
$6.95 CDN, $5.95 US

Piglets Don't Watch Television
1-894222-16-4 available now
$6.95 CDN, $5.95 US

Goldfish Don't Take Bubble Baths
1-894222-10-5 available now
$6.95 CDN, $5.95 US

Puppy's First Year
1-894222-25-3 available now
$8.95 CDN, $7.95 US

Kitty's First Year
1-894222-26-1 available now
$8.95 CDN, $7.95 US

www.lobsterpress.com